IMPRINT

A part of Macmillan Children's Publishing Group

ABOUT THIS BOOK

The illustrations started as original pencil drawings, which were then scanned and digitally colored in Adobe Photoshop. After the color foundation was set, textures were layered onto elements to convey the feel of wood or stone and to achieve a finish that makes you feel as if you can "touch" Tomo's world. The text was set in Futura, and the display type is Kabel and Soko. The book was edited by Erin Stein and designed by Natalie C. Sousa. The production was supervised by Raymond Ernesto Colón, and the production editor was Christine Ma.

Library of Congress Cataloging-in-Publication Data is available.
ISBN 978-1-250-08545-0 (hardcover)

Our books may be purchased in bulk for promotional, educational, or business use. Please contact your local bookseller or the Macmillan Corporate and Premium Sales Department at (800) 221-7945 ext. 5442 or by e-mail at MacmillanSpecialMarkets@macmillan.com.

Imprint logo designed by Amanda Spielman

First Edition—2016
1 3 5 7 9 10 8 6 4 2

mackids.com

Books are meant to love and hold. Buy or borrow, never steal. Heed these words or else one day you'll become a whale's next meal!

FOR ALL THE WORLD'S LITTLE EXPLORERS —T.L.

TREVOR LAI

TOMO

EXPLORES THE WORLD

{Imprint}
MAKE YOUR MARK

New York

On a tiny island far to the north, there lives a young boy.
His name is Tomo, and his life is filled
with one thing: fish.

Fish for breakfast.

Fish for lunch.

Fish for dinner.

Tomo's father is the strongest fisherman in the village. He holds the record for catching the biggest fish.

Tomo's grandfather is the wisest. He knows where and when to find the most fish.

Tomo's great-grandfather was the bravest fisherman. He once rowed straight into a storm to wrestle a fish from the jaws of a toothy shark!

All the villagers say that Tomo will grow up to be the greatest fisherman of all! But Tomo has a secret: He doesn't like to fish.

Tomo and his dog, Captain, stay at home with his grandfather when his father goes away on fishing expeditions. Grandfather loves to tell fishing stories.

As soon as his grandfather falls asleep,
Tomo sneaks away to his secret hideout.

. . . where he gets to do what he really loves: building! Tomo loves to build things with his hands. He works on his inventions every afternoon.

With practice, Tomo learns how to use what he finds around the island to power his inventions. Captain helps him track down what he needs. By using something natural, such as water or sunlight, Tomo brings his creations to life!

The only person who understands Tomo is his best friend, Maya.
She's often busy studying plants and animals,
but she always makes time to admire his inventions.

"My father, grandfather, and great-grandfather are already the best at fishing," Tomo explains to Maya. "I want to do something I can be the best at. Like building! And I want to see the world beyond this island."

The next afternoon, after his grandfather nods off to sleep, Tomo decides to build a boat. But before he begins, he needs a mast for his sail. Then he spots his great-grandfather's fishing rod. It's legendary, it's something no one ever touches— and it's just what he needs!

But as Tomo reaches for the rod, he knocks over his great-grandfather's photo, and out from behind it falls a big red book. It's an Adventure Journal!

In the middle of the book is a giant map. Tomo's great-grandfather
wasn't just a fisherman—he was an explorer, too!
The Adventure Journal has blueprints, drawings, and
a checklist of things to find around the world.
Only some of the boxes are checked off.

GENUS ARCHITEUTHIS

ARIES

W N E
S

PISCES

TAURUS

CETUS

ORION

AQUARIUS

SCULPTOR

CONSTELLATIONS

DISCOVERY CHECKLIST: OCEAN

☑ TOOTH FROM A GREAT WHITE SHARK

☑ FIND THE GENUS ARCHITEUTHIS

☐ HAIR FROM A BABY WHALE

☐ FIND THE GREAT NARWHAL

"If I build these inventions, I can use them to finish the Adventure Journal!"
The next item on the list is a *hair from a baby whale!*

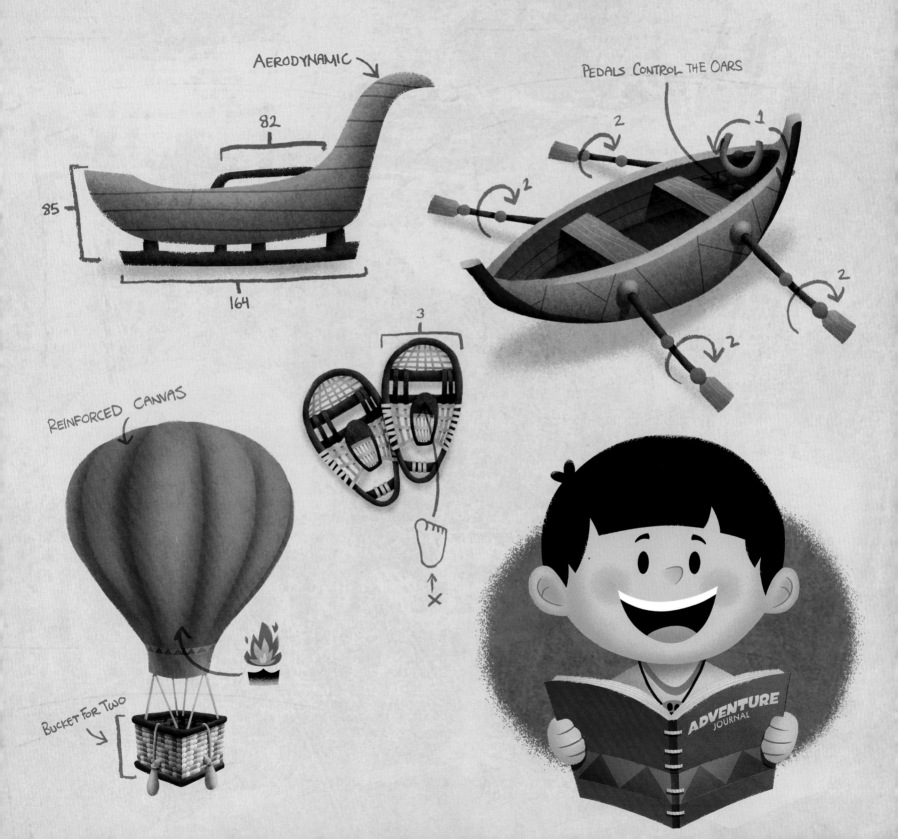

Tomo shows Maya the Adventure Journal and says, "Let's go explore the world."
"I'm pretty busy studying animals today," she says. "Why?"
"When you look up at the sky, what do you see?" he asks.
"I see animals in the clouds!" Maya replies.

"I see a big universe," says Tomo.
"There are lots of animals out there for you to study, too."
Maya thinks for a moment, then nods. "Okay, we can go explore the world.
But I have to be home for dinner."

Tomo follows the blueprint for a canoe in the Adventure Journal to build his boat. Maya also gives him an idea from her animal studies.

Soon they are out at sea.
"Why did you have to bring so many inventions?" asks Maya.
"They might come in handy," says Tomo.
"Shhhh, we have to look for a baby whale."

Tomo, Maya,
and Captain see many
things, but not a baby whale.
Tomo checks the map inside the
Adventure Journal again and again,
but he can't find the exact spot
where the whale is supposed to be.

Maya says, "The stars are coming out. We'd better get home before it's too late. Oh, look! There's the constellation called *Cetus*! That group of stars forms the shape of a whale."

Tomo looks at the map and sees a picture of *Cetus*
right beside the whale drawing. "That's it, Maya!" says Tomo.
"We just need to follow the stars to find the whale!"
Tomo steers the canoe toward the *Cetus* constellation in the sky.

Captain peers into the water and barks.
He sees something!
Tomo waves his oars from side to side, stirring the water.
Suddenly, a huge body emerges from the ocean,
nearly tipping them over!

Then a baby whale surprises Tomo and Maya on the other side of the canoe. The baby whale sheds a tiny hair, and Maya catches it before it can land in the ocean.

They wave farewell to the whales
and follow the stars back to the island.

As they arrive onshore, Tomo's father
is also returning from his fishing trip.
"It looks like you were out fishing. Did you
catch anything today?" his father asks.

"We sure did!" Maya answers happily. "We caught something small but very special," agrees Tomo.

Tomo builds a special clubhouse where he and Maya can plan
their future adventures. Tomo and Maya put away the whale hair
and then check off the item in the Adventure Journal.
"I can't wait to go on our next adventure!" Maya says.
"We're just getting started," Tomo agrees with a smile.

After his fish dinner, Tomo tucks his great-grandfather's book under his pillow and dreams about much more than fish. . . . Tomo dreams about exploring the world.

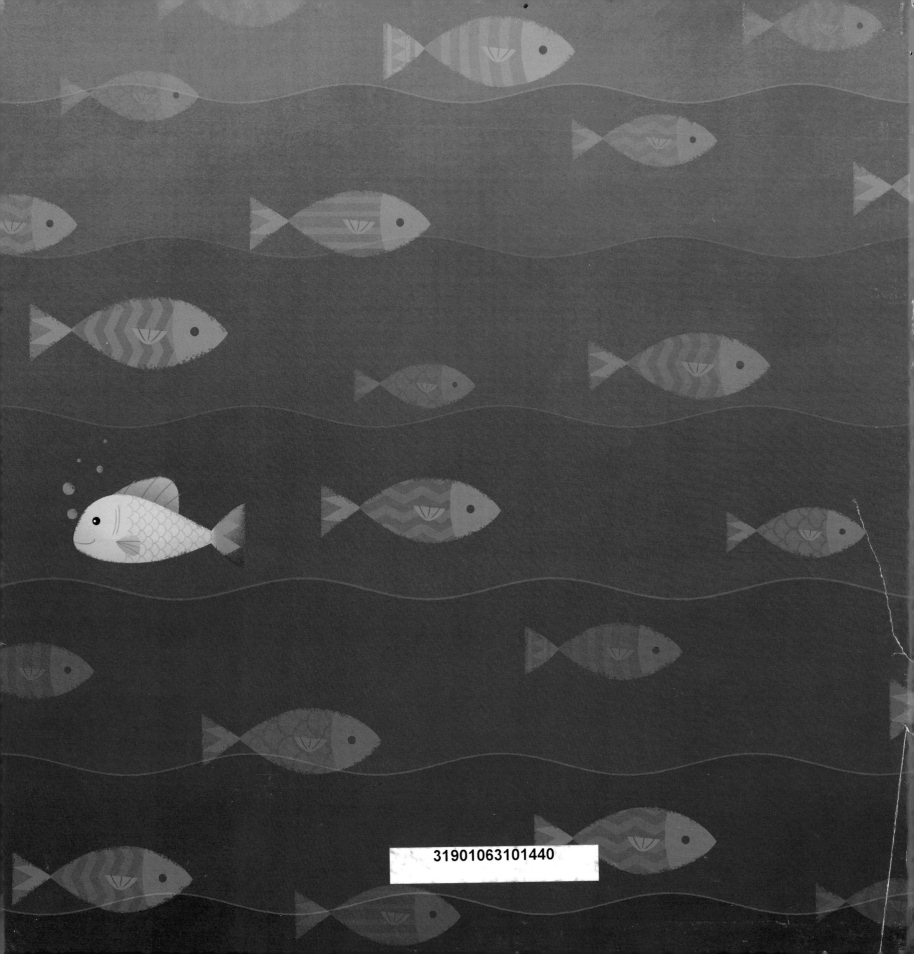